The Secret Rescuers

Maya was so excited she could hardly breathe. She'd never seen a sky unicorn foal before! His legs were slender and his soft coat was so white it almost glowed…

Look out for more
thrilling adventures!

The
STORM
DRAGON

The
LITTLE
FIREBIRD

The
MAGIC
FOX

The Secret Rescuers

The SKY UNICORN

Paula Harrison

illustrated by SOPHY WILLIAMS

nosy crow

 For Imme J-T

First published in the UK in 2015 by Nosy Crow Ltd
The Crow's Nest, 10a Lant St
London, SE1 1QR, UK

Nosy Crow and associated logos are trademarks and/or
registered trademarks of Nosy Crow Ltd

Text copyright © Paula Harrison, 2015
Illustrations © Sophy Williams, 2015

Printed and bound in the UK by Clays Ltd, St Ives Plc

Papers used by Nosy Crow are made from wood grown in sustainable forests.

ISBN: 978 0 85763 496 2

www.nosycrow.com

Chapter One
The Snow White Foal

Maya leaned over the side of the boat and
let her fingers trail through the cool water.
It was wonderful to sail along with the breeze
tickling her cheek and ruffling her long black
hair. She loved watching the ducks swim and
seeing the rabbits scampering along the sandy
bank. The river ran all the way through the
Emerald Plain and there was so much wildlife
to see!

Sometimes, if she was really lucky, Maya
would catch sight of a magical creature.

There were lots of amazing magical animals in the Kingdom of Arramia, like giant eagles with golden feathers, star wolves that sang, and even sky unicorns!

The river sparkled in the sunshine. Two planets, one green and one purple, hung in the cloudless sky.

Leaning out a bit further, Maya watched the six boats following theirs down the river.

Each one had a large white sail and a cabin
painted in bright red, blue and green. Maya and
her family were part of Mr Inigo's Amazing
Travelling Troupe. They sailed up and down
the kingdom's lakes and rivers, stopping in every
town to put on a show. Right now they were on
their way to the town of Blyford on the shores
of Misty Lake.

Maya smiled to herself. She couldn't
wait for the next show. She was
going to perform a new dance
in the turquoise dress
she was wearing.

She'd been practising for weeks!

"Maya, don't lean out too far," said her mum. "You don't want to fall in with that nice dress on!"

Maya moved back a little and smoothed the folds of the turquoise dress. It was made of a silky material that shimmered in the light. "Are we close to Misty Lake yet?"

"It's not far now," her mum replied. "I expect we'll look for a place to camp soon."

Her dad came out of the cabin and took hold of the main rope to pull in the sail. Then he fetched a small silver trumpet and blew a single note. On the next boat, Maya's three older brothers took down their sail. Then they each blew a note on their own silver trumpet. This was how they sent messages down the line of boats. Soon all the sails were in and the boats slowed down a little.

"There's Misty Lake – just beyond the bridge." Her dad pointed to a wooden bridge

not far downstream. A mass of glittering water lay just beyond it.

"I can see it!" Maya made a graceful jump, raising her arms as if they were wings. Then she twirled around. They were moves from her new dance.

"Maya!" Her mum laughed. "Remember, no dancing on the boat. There isn't room!"

"Sorry, I forgot!" Maya stopped herself halfway through the spin.

The boat sailed around a bend in the river and a towering hill came into view. There was a pale shape standing at the top, which made Maya catch her breath.

It was a sky unicorn.

As Maya watched, more unicorns trotted over the brow of the hill, their snowy manes flowing in the breeze. With their white coats, golden horns and brightly coloured tails, they looked like the most beautiful creatures in the whole kingdom!

Maya had seen sky unicorns before, but never so many together. There must have been at least twenty of them! The tallest one at the front lifted his head and his golden horn gleamed in the sunlight. Maya had heard stories about how sky unicorns could gallop into the air and race right through the clouds, but she'd never seen them do it. She watched them eagerly, but the magical animals showed no sign of leaving the hill.

"They're amazing, aren't they?" said her dad. "Now, where did I put the spare mooring rope?"

"I wish they'd fly," sighed Maya. "If I could gallop through the sky I'd do it all the time."

"Perhaps there's a foal," said her mum. "Unicorns will often stay on the ground if there's a foal because the little ones can't fly until they're older. Now, I'd better help your dad find that rope." She hurried away.

The sky unicorns walked slowly down the hill to the river, close to Maya's boat. A little foal

skipped to the front of the herd, his turquoise
tail swishing happily. Then he bent his head
to drink from the river. Maya was so excited
she could hardly breathe. She'd never seen
a unicorn foal before. His legs were slender
and his soft coat was so white it almost glowed.
He raised his head and looked at her with big
dark eyes.

"Hello, I'm Maya!" she called softly.

The foal nodded his head and shook his snowy mane, almost as if he were saying hello back.

Just then, a man riding a horse appeared at the top of the hill. Maya guessed at once that he must be a knight because he was dressed in armour. When he saw the unicorns, he shouted at two guards who were hurrying after him.

Then he drew his sword and rode towards the unicorns. "Stop, you horrible beasts!" he bellowed. "Stop in the name of the queen."

The unicorn foal jumped in fright and his tail trembled.

Maya turned to her parents in alarm, but
they'd both disappeared into the cabin.

The sky unicorns dashed along the riverbank,
scared away by the man's fierce shouting.
The knight chased them, urging his horse to go
faster. The sky unicorns quickened into a gallop.
Racing along the riverbank, they dashed across
the wooden bridge that spanned the river.
Their hooves made a sound
like thunder.

The knight urged his horse to go faster but he couldn't match their speed. "How dare you!" he yelled. "Come back at once! All magical beasts are to be captured by Royal Order." He called to the guards, but they were slowed down by their heavy swords and shields.

Maya watched with wide eyes. Why would *anyone* want to chase a unicorn? The herd had almost reached the end of the bridge now. Soon they would be on the other side of the river. Maya smiled to see them gallop so fast. Then her heart dropped.

Where was the foal?

Quickly, she scanned the bridge and the riverbank. The foal had fallen over beside a bramble patch halfway to the bridge. He was trying to stand up again, but his leg was caught by a prickly branch.

"Mum, Dad, quick!" Maya called, but her parents didn't come out of the cabin. The boats behind theirs were hidden by the

bend in the river so no one else could see what
was happening.

Maya's heart thumped faster. The knight was
riding towards the bridge with his sword in his
hand. Any moment now he might notice the
baby unicorn.

Running to the back of the boat, Maya turned
the ship's wheel to make the boat drift closer to
the bank.

She eyed the water. It was so shallow that
she could see the bottom. She knew she was a
good swimmer anyway.

Climbing on to the side of the boat, she
jumped in.

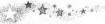

Chapter Two
The Noise in the Dark

Maya landed in the river with a splash. The water reached her waist, soaking through her turquoise dancing dress. It was freezing cold, but there was no time to think about that. The little unicorn needed her help!

The knight was still riding hard with his guards running after him. Their eyes were fixed on the herd of unicorns on the bridge. None of them had spotted the unicorn foal by the bramble patch.

"Come on, Huster! Get a move on, Brinch!"

bellowed the knight. "We're losing them."

The guards tried to run faster, their heavy shields bouncing against their sides. Making sure they weren't looking, Maya waded to the edge of the river and scrambled up the bank.

The little unicorn shivered as she got closer. Maya crouched down, glad that she was hidden from the knight and his guards by the tangle of bushes. "Don't worry!" she whispered to the foal. "I won't hurt you."

The foal gave a soft whinny and gazed at her with big dark eyes.

"What happened?" Maya stroked his snowy mane. "Are you stuck?" She gently checked his hooves and found the bramble caught round his leg.

The foal twitched nervously.

"It's all right," said Maya, carefully untangling his hoof. "There – all done!"

The foal sprang to his feet and skipped around, tossing his head in delight.

Maya peeked over the bushes to check the knight hadn't seen them. She sighed with relief when she saw the men crossing the bridge. But where had the unicorn herd gone?

The knight and his guards reached the other side of the river. They stared all around, as if trying to find the unicorns, before riding away along the road that led to town.

Maya spotted the sky unicorn herd in a little
hidden valley behind a grove of trees near the
water's edge.

"There's your herd!" Maya told the little
unicorn, pointing to the opposite bank. "Can
you find your way?"

The foal seemed to think he could. He
brushed his nose against Maya's hair and then
skipped across the bridge and through the trees
into the hidden valley to join the herd again.

Maya smiled as she watched him. Then she
hurried to the water's edge and waded back to
the boat. Her muddy dress clung to her legs.
Her mum would tell her off for getting messy,
but she didn't mind. She was so glad the foal
was safe again.

Maya was relieved that everyone thought she'd
just paddled in the river for fun. Her mum and
dad had been busy searching for the mooring
rope in the cabin. The rest of the troupe had

sailed round the bend in the river just as the knight had crossed the bridge. They'd been too busy staring at him to look at Maya. She was happy that her meeting with the unicorn foal was her special secret!

"Honestly, Maya!" scolded her mum. "What were you thinking – splashing around in your dancing dress? I don't think I'll be able to wash those mud stains out."

"Sorry, Mum!" Maya said meekly.

The six boats of Mr Inigo's Amazing Travelling Troupe stopped close to the bridge and fastened their mooring ropes. Everyone disembarked and together they built a fire that they could use for cooking. Dinner was to be a stew made with freshly caught fish.

The troupe relaxed around the campfire while the stew was cooking. Everyone was there: the married acrobats Monty and May; Maya's three older brothers – the juggling triplets; the Kittersons, who put on plays; Ruben Gribba the magician; and the grown-up dancers Floella and Daisy, with Daisy's four-year-old daughter, Lucy. Then there was Mr Inigo, who sang opera songs in his splendid deep voice. Maya's parents didn't perform any more, but helped with all the

costumes and sold tickets for the shows.

"This is an excellent place to stop for the night," said Mr Inigo, twirling his long black moustache. "It's only a few minutes' walk into Blyford. Tomorrow we'll go into town to put up posters for our Grand Show!"

"I hope we'll all get a bit more money this time," grumbled Ruben the magician, stroking his long beard. "I hardly got any coins from that last place."

"The coins are always shared out fairly," said Maya's mum. "Perhaps you spent all yours too fast."

Ruben got up, muttering something about measly wages. "I'm going to collect firewood."

Maya stared across the river. Were the unicorns still sheltering among the trees on the other side? It was hard to see now it was growing dark.

"We need some more herbs for the stew," said Maya's dad, stirring the huge pot. "Some mint

and rosemary, I think."

"I'll get them!" said Maya quickly. "I won't
be long." Taking a lantern, she hurried towards
the bridge. She'd look for the unicorns while she
collected the herbs. Maybe she'd even get to see
the little foal again!

Her footsteps sounded loud on the wooden
boards. She watched the river flowing slowly
under the bridge into the huge lake beyond.
When she reached the other side, Maya tiptoed
through the trees into the little valley where the
sky unicorns had hidden.

They were still there. Some were grazing and
others were resting. Their pale coats and manes
shone in the twilight. The little foal was sleeping
next to a larger unicorn and Maya guessed it
must be his mother. She gazed at them for a
while, not wanting to get too close in case she
alarmed them.

A movement near the trees made her turn
round. A figure was creeping away from the

unicorns towards the bridge. It was Ruben Gribba, with his thin face and long beard. Maya wondered if he'd wanted to see the unicorns again too, except he didn't seem the sort of person who liked animals. He hadn't been carrying any firewood either.

Maya watched the unicorns for a while. Then she realised it had got much darker and her dad needed herbs for the stew. She quickly picked some mint leaves.

She was about to cross the bridge when she heard a rushing sound in the air. She peered up into the darkness.

What *was* that? It almost sounded like huge wings beating in the air.

The noise grew louder, ending in a gigantic splash.

Maya followed the sound. She was sure something pretty big must have landed in the water! Then, to her surprise, she heard a girl's voice.

"Windrunner! Did you have to land in the river? I'm soaking wet!"

A long string of growls answered her.

Maya raised her lantern but she couldn't see very far. "Hello?" she said. "Is everyone all right?"

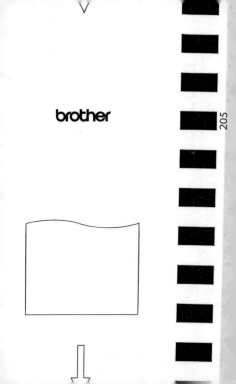

brother

Canon Peter Hall C of E PS

VISITOR

LOUISE HARDY

Parent

Visiting: Rebecca Brown

Tue 10 December 2019

Visitors are required to read and observe the visitors rules, a copy of which is available from reception.

Chapter Three
The Magical Stone

"Who's there?" the girl called back.

"I'm Maya, from Mr Inigo's Amazing Travelling Troupe. Do you need help?" Maya peered into the darkness. She thought she could see two shapes near the water's edge. One of them seemed absolutely huge. There were more growls – quieter this time.

Maya clambered down the bank and then stopped short. A blonde-haired girl was standing by the edge of the river, clutching a small cloth bag. Water dripped from her dress.

Right next to her, shaking water off his wings, was a huge green dragon.

Maya stared at the dragon. He coughed and a little flame spurted out of his mouth.

"Don't be scared. He's really friendly!" said the girl. "Are you all by yourself?"

"Um … yes I am." Maya still couldn't take her eyes off the dragon. She'd seen the creatures flying in the distance before, but she'd never actually *met* one. He was enormous – nearly the size of her boat – and his skin was so scaly.

"You don't mind dragons, do you?" the girl asked eagerly.

"No, not at all!" Maya smiled. Now she'd got over the surprise, it really was very exciting to be so close to a dragon.

She wondered why the girl and the dragon were together. She'd never heard of dragons being friends with humans before.

The girl shaded her eyes from the light of Maya's lantern.

"I'm Sophy and this is my friend Windrunner, the storm dragon. We've flown for miles and miles to get here!"

She clambered up the bank towards Maya, but tripped on some rough ground and fell over.

The little cloth bag flew from her fingers and a handful of stones fell out on to the grass. Sophy gasped and snatched up the bag again immediately.

"Are you all right? Here, I'll help." Maya set the lantern on the ground and began picking up the fallen stones. They were small – each was no bigger than a strawberry. She held one close to the lantern to get a better look. It was grey and lumpy, and not very pretty at all.

Suddenly the stone glowed orange and felt hot against her skin. "Ouch!" She dropped it, afraid it would burn her fingers. "What's happening?"

"Wait!" breathed Sophy. "You'll see…"

Maya's eyes widened as the rock blazed brighter and brighter. With a snap, it broke in half and the orange glow faded. Her fingers trembling, Maya picked up the two pieces of rock. Each one had a tiny hollow inside, filled

with sparkling emerald-green crystals.

"That's amazing!" whispered Maya.

"It's magic and I can show you how it works!"
Sophy smiled widely. "This is fantastic luck!
I didn't think I'd find anyone so quickly."

Maya stared at the other girl, her mind
whirling. She really wasn't sure what Sophy
meant about finding someone. "This stone is
magic? Really?" She looked down at the two
pieces of rock in her hand. The green crystals
glittered.

"Yes, really!" Sophy nodded vigorously. "I
know it must seem strange, but you see, the
same thing happened to me! This is a Speaking
Stone. It lets you talk to magical animals. The
queen threw out this bag of stones as if they
were rubbish after the king died."

"She didn't know they were magical then?"

"No, and she doesn't like magic anyway."
Sophy lifted a thread over her neck. "Your
stone will only work for you. See, I have one of

my own! Now I talk to magical animals all the time." She showed Maya a stone dangling on the end of the thread. It looked rough and grey on the outside like Maya's. Opening the stone, Sophy revealed a little cave of purple crystals.

"So I'll be able to talk to magical animals too?" Maya almost squeaked with excitement.

"Try it now!" Sophy grabbed Maya's hand. "Say something to Windrunner."

Maya faced the dragon and swallowed. "H-hello, Windrunner! I'm pleased to meet you."

Windrunner's amber eyes blinked and he bowed his head. "Pleased to meet you too. Any friend of Sophy's is a friend of the storm dragons!"

Maya gasped. It was just so strange hearing the growling noise from his mouth turn into words.

"You *see*!" Sophy was bouncing on her toes. "It's lucky I found you. The stones only work for

a few people and I really need your help because danger is coming. That's why I'm here!"

"What's the danger?" asked Maya.

"There's a knight at the royal castle who hates magical animals – a really horrible man! He's set out to destroy them and we think he's on his way here. We've spent all day flying around looking for him but we haven't seen him yet."

"I'm very tired from all the flying!" grunted Windrunner. "I will rest a little, Sophy." He blew warm breath on the ground and then settled down with his tail curled around his body.

Sophy and Maya climbed to the top of the riverbank, where the path led to the bridge.

Maya held the two pieces of her magical stone tightly. "But how did you make friends with a dragon?"

"I rescued his baby brother from the castle," explained Sophy. "I work there as a maid. That's how I know Sir Fitzroy – he's the knight I was telling you about—" She broke off as footsteps

sounded on the bridge.

"Maya, is that you?" called her mum. "Are you all right? You've been such a long time that we wondered where you'd got to."

"I'm fine, Mum! Just a minute," Maya called back, before whispering to Sophy, "I'm sorry – I have to go. But I really want to help … and a knight rode past here today. He might be the one you mean."

Sophy nodded. "Meet me here – just underneath the bridge – at first light and we'll work out what to do. Remember your stone only works for you! Don't show it to anyone."

"Don't worry, I won't!" Maya smiled at her new friend before hurrying across the bridge.

So many strange things had happened in one day. First she'd helped the unicorn foal, and then this girl – Sophy – had appeared from nowhere! Now she had a special stone that let her talk to magical animals and *that* was the most amazing thing of all!

Chapter Four
The Town by the Lake

Maya found it hard to sleep that night. She stared up at the drawings of famous dancers pinned on the wall above her cabin bed. Usually the gentle movement of the water underneath the boat helped her to sleep, but tonight her mind was full of sky unicorns and magical stones.

Just before dawn she got up and took the special stone from under her pillow. Fetching a thread from the sewing basket, Maya tied the two pieces together. Then she made the thread

into a necklace and hung it round her neck as
Sophy did. The stone was hidden beneath her
dress where no one would see it.

Then she tiptoed out of the cabin and
climbed to shore. Feeling a little shy, she crossed
the bridge to find Sophy and Windrunner.

Sophy was already waiting for her. "Are those
your boats?" She pointed across the river.

"Yes, we travel along the rivers and lakes
putting on shows in each town." Maya forgot
her shyness as she told Sophy all about the
different acts in their show.

Sophy was especially interested in Maya's
dancing. Then she told Maya about life in the
castle and her troubles with the wicked knight,
Sir Fitzroy.

Maya nodded. "He sounds just like the
knight I saw yesterday." And she explained to
Sophy how he'd chased the sky unicorns before
galloping towards Blyford.

Sophy's cheeks flushed. "Horrible man! If he

took the path to town we should follow him and see if we can find out what his plan is."

Windrunner lumbered up the riverbank and yawned, showing rows of glistening teeth. Then he shook his tail and stretched his leathery wings. "If you are venturing into the human town then I must leave you for now, dear Sophy," he said. "I'll scare the townspeople if I fly too close to their houses. Send a golden songbird to find me when you need me again."

"Thanks, Windrunner." Sophy hugged him.

The huge green dragon launched into the air and flew away across Misty Lake. Maya watched him soar upwards, amazed at how fast he could fly. She noticed how the wind gusted and the clouds swirled as the dragon flew away.

Sophy's stomach rumbled. "I didn't realise I was so hungry."

"I'll bring us some breakfast," said Maya. "And I'll fetch the show posters. Pinning them up gives me a good reason for going to town."

 34

Quickly, Maya fetched some blueberry scones and a handful of the posters. The girls sat on a tree stump and munched their breakfast.

"Thanks, Maya!" Sophy beamed. "These are delicious."

Maya smiled back a little shyly. There was something she really wanted to ask. She just hoped Sophy wouldn't mind. "Do you think … have we got time to look at the sky unicorns before we go to town?"

Sophy glanced at the sun rising in the sky. "I'd love to see them too. We can be quick, can't we?"

Maya nodded eagerly. "They're in a hidden valley not very far away – I'll show you!" She led Sophy away from the bridge. They crept through the trees and down the slope into the little dell that Maya had visited the evening before.

Many of the unicorns were awake and grazing quietly. They raised their heads as the girls tiptoed closer, and their golden horns gleamed in the sunlight. Then, when they saw that it was Maya and Sophy, they went back to nibbling the grass again.

"Aren't they beautiful?" whispered Sophy, her blue eyes shining. "I guess you've seen sky unicorns before, but I've lived in the castle my whole life. I've seen plenty of royal banquets and golden crowns, but I've never seen anything as amazing as these creatures!"

"I never saw them close up till yesterday," said Maya. "Look, there's the little foal!"

The baby unicorn left his mother and gambolled around the dell, flicking his little tail. Maya crouched down and held out her hand. The foal tossed his snowy mane and gazed at her. Then at last he trotted up and gently nibbled her fingers.

Maya's heart leapt. She'd hardly dared hope that she would get so close to him again and now the magical stone gave her the chance to talk to him too!

She swallowed. "Hello, my name's Maya. Don't be afraid – I have a magical stone that lets me talk to you."

The foal looked startled and took a few steps back. Then he crept closer again. "My name's Clover," he said in a soft, high whinny. "Thank you for helping me yesterday!"

"You're welcome!" Maya smiled.

Clover danced forward and nibbled at her hair, before galloping off around the valley again.

"What a sweet little foal," said Sophy. "Come on, let's go into town and see if Sir Fitzroy is there. I'm determined that he shan't have the chance to harm any magical creatures."

The girls left the tiny hidden valley and followed the path to town. Blyford was a large

place with bustling streets and a town square in the middle.

Sophy gazed round. "I've never been to a town this big before! You must be used to all this because of travelling around on the boat. You live an amazing life!"

"You live in the royal castle!" said Maya. "That's pretty awesome!"

"Well, I do like polishing the queen's tiaras," said Sophy, laughing.

Maya giggled too. She couldn't help liking Sophy. She was so chatty and had a warm smile. There were lots of questions she wanted to ask her, like how many tiaras did the queen have? And how had Sophy rescued the little dragon? And when Sophy was flying on Windrunner's back, wasn't she afraid of falling off?

She was just wondering what to ask first when she saw a man in silver armour on the other side of the town square. "That's the man who chased the unicorns!" she said to Sophy.

"Is he your horrid knight?"

Sophy shivered. "Yes, that's Sir Fitzroy. I wonder what he's up to."

The girls crossed the square, weaving in and out of the fruit sellers and stalls full of shoes and hats. A tall lady dressed in a dark-red cloak came out of a grand building and walked down the steps to shake the knight's hand.

"That's the leader of Blyford walking out of the Town Hall," muttered Maya. "Her name's Dame Gibson."

Maya and Sophy edged closer to the steps and then stopped to look at a hat stall. They pretended they were interested in buying a purple hat. It gave them the chance to listen to Sir Fitzroy's conversation.

"Greetings, Sir Fitzroy," said Dame Gibson. "We haven't seen you in Blyford for many years. What brings you to our town?"

"I'm hunting down every magical beast in this kingdom," snarled Sir Fitzroy. "Her Majesty,

Queen Viola, was nearly killed by a dragon
attack on her own castle two days ago. It's time
we sorted out these disgusting creatures once
and for all."

Chapter Five
Mr Inigo's Show Begins

Maya glanced over her shoulder at Sir Fitzroy, who was still talking to the town leader. "Was there really a dragon attack?" she murmured to Sophy.

"No!" Sophy whispered back. "There was one poor baby dragon who wanted to go home."

Dame Gibson shook her head. "I'm shocked, Sir Fitzroy! Here in Blyford we've always loved magical animals. Many creatures like sky unicorns roam the Emerald Plain. I can't believe they deserve such harsh treatment."

"You can say what you like but you'll have to obey Royal Orders like everyone else," growled Sir Fitzroy, unrolling a scroll of paper with the mark of a crown. "Now, where do these sky unicorns live? I saw them yesterday but the wretched things sneaked away. I command you to show me where they are."

Dame Gibson shook her head. "I'm afraid I can't. People say that the sky unicorns have favourite places where they like to graze, but there are lots of little valleys on the Emerald Plain. They could be anywhere!"

Someone coughed just behind Maya. Turning her head, she thought she recognised the man behind her, but he disappeared into the crowd before she could be sure.

"Look, Maya!" Sophy nudged her. "Is that your travelling troupe?"

A murmur of excitement ran through the town square as Mr Inigo swept in wearing the multicoloured patchwork cloak that he put on

for each show. Behind him were the acrobats, as well as Maya's brothers – the jugglers – and the dancers, Floella and Daisy.

Maya suddenly remembered that she was supposed to have put up posters for the show. She quickly ran to pin them on the nearby walls.

"Roll up! Roll up!" called Mr Inigo, twirling his moustache. "Come and see some acts from our show for free. Then buy tickets for our spectacular Grand Show tonight!"

"Maya, we need you." Maya's brother Rick tapped her shoulder. "Mr Inigo's decided to set up right here and show the crowd a few of our acts so that they buy tickets for the main performance. We need you to dance."

"All right then!" Maya felt a fizzing in her tummy. Dancing in front of a crowd was always exciting and a little bit scary.

"I'll watch you – good luck!" said Sophy.

The acrobats, Monty and May, laid out dancing mats and tied a ribbon around eight poles to keep the performance area clear. The crowd pressed forward, eager to see.

"Maya!" Floella dashed over and handed Maya her dance shoes. "Start with your freestyle routine and finish with the ballet dance. Mr Inigo will play the music for you."

"Thanks, Floella." Maya put on her dancing shoes and smoothed her long dark hair.

Mr Inigo held up his hands for silence. "And first, I'd like to introduce one of our youngest and best dancers. Please give a round of applause for the Magnificent … the Marvellous … the Magical Maya!"

The crowd clapped wildly. Maya blushed and got into her starting position with her legs straight and her arms high above her head. Her heart was racing as Mr Inigo began to play a tune on his violin.

As soon as she started to dance, Maya forgot to be nervous. She sometimes wondered how she could dance in front of a crowd when she often felt so shy. The music seemed to set her free. She leapt and spun to the beat, and the crowd began to clap in time with the music.

Maya finished her first dance and dropped a curtsy, blushing again at the cheers from the townspeople.

Sophy was standing right at the front. "Well done, Maya!" she called. "You were great!"

Mr Inigo twirled his moustache again and then struck up a slower melody. This was the music for Maya's favourite ballet dance. Pointing her toes, she moved to the music and leapt gracefully across the floor. Then she swayed and twirled, before moving into a beautiful arabesque.

As she turned to repeat her movements, something caught her eye. The knight, Sir Fitzroy, was still standing on the steps. He was frowning as if he wasn't enjoying the performance at all. Then a figure slipped out of the crowd and joined him.

Ruben Gribba, the magician, muttered in Sir Fitzroy's ear. A nasty smile spread across the knight's face, which turned Maya's heart cold. The movement of the dance took her in the other direction. When she turned back again, Sir Fitzroy was giving Ruben a handful of gold

coins. Then the two men walked down the steps together and disappeared behind the crowd.

Maya carried on dancing but an icy dread rose inside her. What had Ruben done? She pictured him the evening before, watching the unicorns grazing in their hidden valley. Was it possible he'd told the horrible knight where to find them? She wanted to run after the two men but she was in the middle of a dance and everyone was watching. What was she supposed to do?

She kept on going till the end and tried to smile as the crowd applauded her. Then, when Mr Inigo announced the next act, Maya slipped away and found Sophy. "Quickly!" she gasped. "The knight's gone! I think Ruben's told him where to find the sky unicorns."

"Who's Ruben?" said Sophy.

"He belongs to our troupe. He was talking to Sir Fitzroy. Then they both disappeared really fast."

The girls struggled to get through the crowd.
They reached the edge of the square, but for a
moment Maya couldn't remember which street
to follow. At last she recognised the right one
and the girls ran until their legs ached. They
stopped where the houses ended, trying to catch
their breath.

"It'll take us too long to get back to the
bridge," said Sophy. "If Sir Fitzroy's riding his
horse he could be there already!"

Maya looked around desperately. She pictured
Clover galloping round the hidden valley, his
turquoise tail flying. She couldn't let Sir Fitzroy
hurt him. There had to be a way to get there
faster.

They were close to the waterfront where
the boats were moored. Maya noticed her
brothers' boat tied to the jetty. They must have
sailed up here with the dancing mats and other
equipment.

"We'll catch up with them if we go by boat,"

she told Sophy. "This one belongs to my brothers. Come on, let's go!"

Sophy climbed aboard while Maya untied the mooring rope. Then they pushed off from the jetty and hoisted the sail. Maya wished she could have asked her family for help, but if Sir Fitzroy discovered they'd gone against Royal Orders they'd all be in terrible trouble. She and Sophy would have to help the sky unicorns without anyone finding out.

The wind whistled across the lake, whipping up little waves. Maya turned the wheel and the boat sped up at once. They glided up the lake towards the river just as Sir Fitzroy and Ruben Gribba rode on to the bridge. The knight got off his horse and took out a small telescope to peer closely at the riverbank. Ruben pointed in the direction of the hidden valley and Sir Fitzroy mounted his horse again before they rode off together.

"Now what?" said Sophy. "Shall we get to the shore?"

Maya's forehead creased. "We're still going to be too late. We have to let the unicorns know they're in danger!"

She dived into the cabin, rummaging under her brothers' things. She threw juggling sticks and beanbags aside. She flung odd socks and orange peel out of her way. Then she found what she wanted – a gleam of silver under all the mess.

"Found it!" She drew out a large silver trumpet. "We're going to warn the sky unicorns without anyone ever knowing it was us."

Chapter Six
The Silver Trumpet

"Will it work?" Sophy eyed the trumpet doubtfully.

"It makes a really horrible noise every time I try to play it. I'm sure it would scare any animal! There might be some drums in there too. See if you can find them." Maya dashed back to the deck.

The boat had glided closer to the bridge with its narrowly spaced pillars.

"Sophy!" called Maya. "Can you help me with the sail? We'll have to take it down to get

under the bridge."

"Sure!" Sophy ran out carrying a red-and-white drum and two beaters. "What do I need to do?"

Maya showed her which rope lowered the main sail. Sophy put down the drum and together they heaved and heaved until the white sail came down. Then they tied the rope firmly in place.

"Help me with the wheel!" said Maya.

Together the girls held the wheel steady as they glided under the bridge. Maya held her breath. Going wrong here would send them crashing into the pillars that held up the bridge! A moment later, they passed safely into the sunshine on the other side. Then they turned the boat towards the shore where the unicorn's hidden valley met the water's edge.

Glimpses of white coats and golden horns could be seen between the trees. Maya felt excitement rising inside her. The sky unicorns

were still there. She and Sophy had made it in time. Two unicorns with purple tails raised their heads as the boat zoomed into view.

"Run away!" Sophy called to the creatures. "Danger's coming!" But the wind whipped the words from her mouth and the unicorns were too far away to understand.

Maya lifted the silver trumpet to her lips. She had to get this right. It had to be a really loud sound to scare the sky unicorns away. Taking a deep breath, she blew into the instrument.

All that came out was a funny blowing noise, like an elephant with a cold.

"Try again!" urged Sophy. "Maybe you need

to blow harder."

Maya pushed her hair out of her eyes and
blew again. This time she made a deep, harsh
sound. The unicorns looked up, their tails
swishing anxiously, but they didn't run away.

Taking a huge breath, Maya blew again.

This time she made a noise so horrible that
Sophy put her hands over her ears. "That
sounds *totally* awful!" she shouted over the din.
"I'll join in with the drum." Grabbing the drum,
she banged it very fast with the beaters.

The sky unicorns sprang away, galloping
across the little valley.

"Look, they're leaving!" cried Sophy. "Well done, Maya. That noise was terrible."

Maya beamed as she watched the sky unicorns disappearing through the trees. Then she saw a shadow moving on the other side of the valley. She ducked down behind a big coil of rope, pulling Sophy with her.

Sir Fitzroy marched down the steep slope, scowling deeply. He turned to shout something, but the girls were too far away to hear what it was.

"As soon as he's gone, we'll go back under the bridge," said Maya, and Sophy nodded.

Sir Fitzroy strode up and down the hidden valley a few times. Maya noticed him staring over at the boat but she knew that she and Sophy couldn't be seen. She hoped that the knight would give up on finding the sky unicorns. The Emerald Plain was a huge place, stretching hundreds of miles. If the unicorns were out of sight, he'd never find them.

The gentle movement of the river swept the
boat along and the valley started to disappear
from view. Maya got ready to leap for the wheel
as soon as she had the chance. She glanced at
the hidden valley one more time and gasped in
horror.

Ruben prowled down the slope to join Sir
Fitzroy. He was holding a creature tightly round
its middle. The little animal was wriggling its
legs but Ruben wouldn't let go. It had a snow-
white coat and a turquoise tail.

Clover had been captured.

"No!" gasped Maya. "Not Clover!"

"Poor little thing!" cried Sophy. "He must
have been slower to gallop away than the
others."

Maya leaned out, desperately trying to see
what was happening, but the river swept the
boat on. The men and the little unicorn foal
disappeared from sight.

Tears pricked Maya's eyes. "This is awful!

How could Ruben be so mean? Clover's only a baby unicorn."

Sophy's cheeks flushed with anger. "They're both very bad men. What shall we do? Get the boat to shore right here and steal Clover back?"

Maya bit her lip. "That could be tricky. They're much bigger than us! Let's follow them and then we can work out a plan."

They sailed over to the riverbank and tied the boat up next to the bridge. Sneaking through the bushes, they saw the men just as they were tying a rope around Clover's neck. Ruben Gribba mounted his horse. Sir Fitzroy also climbed into his saddle and cantered towards Blyford, while the little unicorn was pulled along behind.

"He's taking Clover back to town," whispered Maya. "Maybe he's hoping to use him to lure the other unicorns into danger."

Sophy nodded. "That's exactly the kind of thing Sir Fitzroy would do."

The girls followed at a safe distance. Maya thought of how Clover had gambolled across the grass that morning with his white mane flying. Her heart ached to see him being dragged along with a rope around his neck.

Clover's head drooped and he stumbled as they reached town, but Sir Fitzroy only shouted at him and jerked the rope.

They stopped outside an inn called The Rotten Cauliflower. Sir Fitzroy's guards rushed up to him. The knight yelled some orders and one of the men took the horse to the stables while the other led the foal inside. Then Sir Fitzroy gave more gold coins to Ruben, who walked away stroking his beard and looking very pleased with himself.

Maya felt a lump in her throat as she watched Clover being led away. She couldn't believe Ruben had been so heartless and given away the unicorns' hiding place for a few coins. Worst of all, he'd taken Clover away from his family. She'd never thought he would be so mean.

"Sir Fitzroy must be staying here tonight," she said to Sophy. "We'll have to get inside to rescue Clover."

"How?" Sophy whispered back. "They'll know as soon as they see us that we're not supposed to be there."

Maya thought hard. "I know a way we can do it. We'll just need to borrow a few things. Let's go – we haven't got much time!"

Chapter Seven
The Two Pageboys

Maya rushed down the street to the town square with Sophy close behind her. She was glad to see that Floella and Daisy were still there, packing the dancing costumes into a small wagon.

"Hello, Maya!" said Floella cheerfully. "I meant to tell you how good your dancing was today but I couldn't see you after the show."

"Thank you!" Maya would normally have been delighted to be praised by Floella, who'd taught her every dance step she knew. But right now all she could think of was rescuing Clover.

"Sophy and I left the square after I'd danced," she admitted. "And I need to ask you a favour."

Floella looked at her with wise brown eyes. "Go on! What is it?"

Maya put on her most pleading expression. "We need to borrow the two pageboys' costumes. It's for a ... sort of prank. Please can we?"

Floella jerked her head towards the wagon. "I'm afraid those are right at the bottom of the costume pile."

"Don't worry! I'll get them without messing anything up." Maya climbed into the wagon and slid through the layers of shoes and dresses and cloaks. She came out with two pageboy coats in velvety dark red with gold buttons, two pairs of black trousers and two dark-red caps.

"Don't tear them!" said Floella with a pretend scowl.

"We won't!" said Maya and Sophy together.

On the way back to the inn, they bought a piece of parchment paper from one of the market stalls and rolled it up into a scroll shape. It didn't look perfect, Maya thought, but it would have to do.

It was hard finding a place to change into their costumes but in the end they found an empty part of the stables. They hid their other clothes behind a bale of hay.

Maya tucked her long dark hair under the velvet cap and turned to look at Sophy, dressed in the dark-red uniform. "You look funny!"

Sophy grinned. "So do you! And what's the scroll of paper for?"

"It's a fake message from the queen. It should be enough to get us inside at least."

Sophy's smile was replaced by an anxious frown. "Are you sure this will work? I'm not really used to disguises and pretending to be someone else."

"Don't worry! We've got actors in our troupe and I've watched them putting on plays lots of times," said Maya, pulling her cap low. "Just follow my lead." Her stomach tumbled as they left the stables but she tried to ignore it. Clover was depending on her and she wasn't going to let him down.

The girls marched up to the inn and rapped on the door. One of Sir Fitzroy's guards opened it. "You can't come in," he said roughly. "The

whole inn is reserved for my master—"

"We have a message for Sir Fitzroy from the queen," interrupted Maya, showing him the scroll of paper. "So you'd better let us through."

The guard stared at them for a moment. Maya kept her eyes down, crossing her fingers that they looked like pageboys.

"He's upstairs having dinner," the guard said at last. "It's the second door on the left."

"Thank you!" Maya marched in and climbed the stairs with Sophy close behind her. Luckily, the guard didn't follow them.

"There he is!" whispered Sophy.

The door to Sir Fitzroy's room was open a little. They could see him sitting at the table, his plate piled high with food. He was talking to the second guard. "So tomorrow we'll find out what makes the sky unicorn so *magical*." He said this last word as if it was disgusting. "Then we'll use the little beast to capture the rest of them."

Maya's heart sank. There was no time to lose!

But where had they put Clover?

Tiptoeing along the corridor, she listened at each door. There was no noise behind any of them. Then she heard a faint crying coming from the end of the passage where the stairway led up to the next floor.

Beckoning Sophy, she hurried up the steps. It was dark at the top and it took a few moments for her eyes to get used to the dim light. The crying sounded louder. Following the noise, Maya ran to the last room and pushed open the door.

Clover was trapped inside a small metal cage that stood on the bare floor. "I want my mum," he sobbed. "It's horrible up here. I'm hungry!"

Maya dashed over to the cage. "Shh! Don't cry!" she begged. "It's me – Maya!"

The little foal stopped crying in surprise and whinnied, "Maya! You look different! What are you doing here?"

"We've come to rescue you, of course!" Maya told him. "Oh, Clover! I'm sorry you got caught. Sir Fitzroy is such a horrid man!"

"Maya, I'll keep a lookout," said Sophy, pulling the door closed. "I'll knock if anyone comes."

"You really came to help me?" said Clover, starting to cheer up. "And you speak sky unicorn too!"

"Do you remember the stone I showed you?" Maya pulled out the stone that was hidden under her costume. "I can talk to you because of this. It has magic inside it."

"Like me!" said Clover eagerly. "I have magic inside me."

Maya smiled. "Just like you. Now, how does

this cage open?" She studied the cage but couldn't see a lock or a key. At last she found a little catch on one side but it wouldn't open.

Curling her fingers through the bars, she tugged harder. The catch pinged open. A sharp metal point on the end of the catch scraped across her finger and cut her skin.

"Ouch!" Maya looked at the cut. "Never mind! At least now you can come out of this awful cage."

Clover stepped free from the metal bars and flicked his tail in delight. Then he bent his little head close to Maya's hand. "Let me help you, Maya! This is our secret magic. We never show it to anybody, but I will share it with you!"

Maya watched in astonishment as the little unicorn bent his golden horn to touch her finger. Slowly, the cut on her hand healed until it looked as if it had never been there at all.

"That's amazing!" breathed Maya. "Thank you."

"You're welcome." Clover gently nibbled her hair.

Maya threw her arms around him and his snowy coat felt soft against her cheek. Then she let go and sprang up. "Now, we *must* get you out of here."

There was a quiet rapping on the door. Maya froze. That was Sophy's signal to say that someone was coming.

Creeping to the door, Maya heard a man's voice and footsteps on the stairs. Someone was climbing the steps and it could be Sir Fitzroy. How would they get Clover to safety now?

Chapter Eight
Clover Takes a Leap

Maya's mind whirled. What should she do? Try to hide Clover under her jacket? But he was far too big for that.

There was nothing in the room that would help her either – just a table and a chair. She ran to the window and swung it open. The streets of Blyford were far below. The sun had set now and people were lighting the lamps.

An idea leapt to the front of her mind. "Clover!" she said eagerly. "I know sky unicorns learn to fly – can you do that yet?"

Clover shook his head sadly. "I'm too young to learn. My mum told me I can start flying when I'm older."

The footsteps outside drew nearer.

"What are you doing here, boy?" Sir Fitzroy's voice could be heard outside the door. "You must be up to no good if you're hanging around in the dark."

"I was just looking for the right room, sir," replied Sophy. "I came here with the other pageboy to deliver a letter but we ... got a bit lost."

Clover began shivering at the sound of the knight's voice. Maya knelt down and put her arms round the foal's neck. "Clover," she whispered. "Would you try to fly? Just for me!"

Clover nodded. Then he took a few steps backward, a look of concentration on his little face. Maya smiled in encouragement but her stomach lurched as she heard the knight speaking outside the door again.

"What are you talking about?" Sir Fitzroy snapped at Sophy. "I haven't seen any letter."

Clover cantered into the middle of the room and began galloping in circles, faster and faster. The air sparkled around his hooves. Maya moved over to give him more space but just as she started to feel hopeful, the little foal stopped.

His head drooped. "It's not working, Maya! I'm not flying."

Maya bit her lip. She could hear Sophy still talking to Sir Fitzroy outside the door. Her friend was starting to sound desperate.

"What's going on in there? Stand aside, boy!" barked Sir Fitzroy.

"I know you can do it, Clover!" whispered Maya. "Think of your family flying.

Remember the magic inside you!"

Clover cantered a little but then stopped again. "I don't know! What if I really can't do it?"

"Please, Clover!" cried Maya, not caring any more if Sir Fitzroy heard her. "I believe in you!"

The little foal tossed his mane and began galloping round and round again. This time his hooves sparkled more brightly, as if they were sprinkled with stardust. Then, with one joyful leap, he sprang into the air and galloped right across the room without his hooves touching the floor.

"Fly, Clover, fly!" cheered Maya.

Clover gave an excited whinny and cantered straight out of the window.

The door was wrenched open and Sir Fitzroy marched over to the empty cage. "Where's the beast? Wicked boy, you've ruined my plan!"

Maya was barely listening. Leaning out of the window, she watched Clover dash away into the night sky. He looked so beautiful, galloping beneath the stars. His white mane and turquoise tail lifted in the breeze and a silvery trail sparkled where his hooves had been.

Maya's heart danced as she watched him. Then she frowned a little as he dipped lower.

Was Clover all right? Was flying too hard
for him?

Sir Fitzroy had finally worked out where
Clover had gone. He pushed Maya aside in fury.
"Sneaky animal!" he growled.

Maya saw Sophy beckoning from the doorway. She crept after her friend, glad that the knight was too busy glaring out of the window to notice them escaping. They raced down two flights of stairs and out into the street.

Sophy ran to grab their clothes from the stables. "Clover's doing so well!" she said breathlessly.

"He's very brave, but it's the first time he's ever tried to fly." Maya stared upwards, trying to spot the little unicorn. "What if he gets tired? He could hurt himself if he crashes into a rooftop."

"There he is!" Sophy pointed and the girls began to run.

There were shouts behind them as the guards gave chase.

The girls ran faster, dodging through streets and round corners. Clover cantered through the air, but his hooves dipped lower and lower.

Maya was certain he was getting tired. Surely

they would reach the edge of town soon. Then Clover could land safely.

A few people stopped on the street to gaze up at the unicorn dashing through the night sky. They murmured in wonder at the glittering trail left behind by his hooves.

At last they could see the edge of the town. Clover plunged lower and the girls ran to meet him.

"Careful, Clover!" called Maya. "Go steady!"

"I'm falling!" whinnied the foal.

Stretching out her hands, Maya ran beneath him. He bumped down into her arms, knocking them both to the ground.

Maya giggled. "Clover, you're squashing me and your tail is tickling my nose!"

Sophy helped them both up. "Are you all right?"

"Yes, I'm fine," said Maya. "Are you OK, Clover?"

The little unicorn danced around with his ears

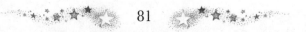

pricked up and his tail swishing. "I flew! Did you see me? I really flew!"

"We saw you and we're really proud of you!" Sophy patted his snowy coat.

Maya cast a quick look behind her. "We need to keep going. Then we'll find a way to get you back to your herd, Clover."

Together, they ran past the last few houses and the lakeside jetty. Then Maya found a place for them to hide behind a clump of bushes. Sir Fitzroy's guards ran past, looking out of breath.

The men searched the path and peered at the lake, but after a few minutes they gave up and went back into town.

Sophy peeked out. "They've gone at last!"

Clover gave a whinny of delight and jumped
out of the bushes.

Maya laughed and hugged him. "You were
very brave," she told him. "Flying for the very
first time must have been really scary."

Clover nuzzled her shoulder. "It was at first,
but you helped me." He gambolled up to Sophy
and nuzzled her shoulder too. "Now I am
Clover the Fabulous Flying Foal!"

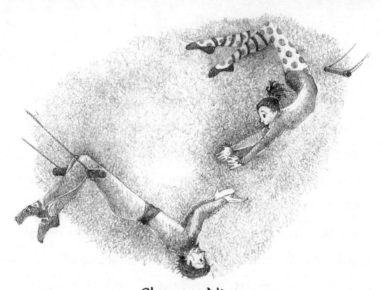

Chapter Nine
The Grand Show

When they reached the bridge, Maya and Sophy changed back into their normal clothes and they all stopped for a rest. Clover sat quietly on the grass, looking tired after all the excitement.

"Why don't we get Windrunner to help us search for the unicorn herd," suggested Sophy. "He'll take us up into the air. It'll be so much easier to find them."

"Good idea," said Maya. "The Emerald Plain is such a huge place. We might get lost in the dark."

Sophy called a golden songbird by whistling
a special tune that Windrunner the dragon had
taught her. She explained to Maya that the
songbirds carried messages for the other magical
animals. Soon one of the golden birds heard
her call. It flew down to perch on her hand and
looked at her with bright black eyes.

"Please could you ask Windrunner the storm dragon to meet me here?" asked Sophy.

"Of course!" The bird stretched its golden feathers and swooped away.

"It'll probably take Windrunner a while to fly here," said Sophy.

"Why don't you both stay here and I'll fetch us something to eat." Maya sprang to her feet and picked up the pageboy costumes.

"Yes, please! I am very hungry," said Clover, resting his head on Sophy's lap.

Maya crossed the bridge and hurried back to camp. She was a little worried that she would be asked to explain exactly what she'd been doing all day. She knew her family would love Clover, but she certainly didn't want to get them into trouble with Sir Fitzroy if he came asking questions later. Also, Maya knew that the troupe would be getting ready for the Grand Show that evening.

When she reached the camp, she was

surprised to find the troupe gathered round the
fire. Maya's triplet brothers were arguing with
an angry-looking Ruben. Maya frowned. She
couldn't forget how nasty Ruben had been to
poor Clover.

"I tell you I didn't take your boat!" said Ruben
furiously.

"It must have been you," said Joe.

"You disappeared for ages this morning,"
said Ben.

"And you came back looking guilty," added
Rick.

"It wasn't me!" snapped Ruben.

"Then why was it tied up by the bridge
instead of where we left it in town?" asked Joe.

Maya gasped. She was the one who had
borrowed her brothers' boat. She was just about
to own up when Ruben burst out, "I tell you, it
wasn't me! I was busy showing that knight where
the sky unicorns were hiding because…" He
tailed off, suddenly aware of everyone frowning

at him. "I just did it to be helpful."

"You did it for the money!" Maya burst out.
"I saw the knight handing you some coins
afterwards."

"Well, so what if you did?" sneered Ruben.
"It's none of your business anyway."

"You didn't care about the unicorns at all!"
Maya's cheeks went bright red. "And you didn't
care about the little foal you took away from his
mother."

"Is this true, Maya?" Her mum got up and
took her daughter's hand.

Maya nodded. "I was with my new friend,
Sophy. We both saw what he did."

Maya's mum rounded on Ruben. "You should
be ashamed of yourself!"

Ruben's eyes glittered. "I deserved that
money!" He pointed at Maya. "And she is just a
horrible little sneak!"

All the members of the troupe started talking
loudly at once.

"Take that back!" Maya's brothers yelled at Ruben.

"Magical animals should never be treated so cruelly," said Floella, shaking her head.

Mr Inigo rose and held up his hand for silence. "Ruben, it's clear that you do not deny what Maya has said. I'm afraid there's no place in our troupe for someone who has abandoned what's right and wrong for the sake of money."

"But..." spluttered Ruben.

"You must go," said Mr Inigo, and the other members of the troupe nodded in agreement.

"Fine! I don't want to stay with you anyway." Ruben glared round at all of them, before marching away to pack his things.

Maya put the pageboy costumes back where they belonged. Then she fetched some small fruit pies, and some lettuce and carrots for Clover, and ran back to the other side of the river.

"Yum!" Clover bounded up to Maya and tugged the vegetables from her hands.

"Thanks, Maya. This is delicious!" said Sophy, nibbling a fruit pie. "The songbird came back while you were gone. Windrunner will be here at dawn. We can rest till then."

"Actually, it's the Grand Show tonight. I nearly forgot because I was thinking so hard about rescuing Clover," explained Maya. "I should really go and dance. I don't want to let the troupe down."

"Have a wonderful time!" beamed Sophy. "We'll be fine here. Won't we, Clover?"

Clover nodded as he chomped on another carrot.

Mr Inigo's Amazing Travelling Troupe put on a spectacular show that night. Maya's brothers juggled with glow sticks. Monty and May did rows of somersaults until the crowd gasped and clapped. Then Floella and Daisy performed a ribbon dance, twirling and spinning their long purple ribbons.

Maya joined the two grown-up dancers for their final number. Her pale-blue dress floated around her as she leapt and spun. Then she performed a beautiful ballet dance by herself. As the music played, she lifted her arms and pointed her toes, enjoying every step. The crowd clapped loudly when she finished and they called for an encore. Maya blushed and made another curtsy. She was so happy they'd loved her dancing!

Finally, Monty and May climbed the tall towers that had been put up on either side of the arena. Climbing on to their trapeze swings, they began to glide through the air. Maya always loved watching their act. It was awesome seeing them soar so high.

Suddenly, her heart fluttered. She would be riding on a dragon for the very first time tonight. The acrobats were flying high on their trapeze but she would be going even higher!

Chapter Ten
Maya's First Flight

After the show was over, and all the costumes
and equipment packed away, Maya told her
mum and dad about her plan.

"Sophy and I are going to take Clover, the
unicorn foal, back to his herd," she said. "We're
going to … um … ride on a dragon to get
there!" She crossed her fingers, hoping her
parents wouldn't say she wasn't allowed.

"You're old enough to be sensible,
Maya," said her mum. "As long as you let
us know where you are and remember to

thank the dragon."

"Your grandmother used to say she'd once ridden a dragon," said her dad. "She was an acrobat. I think she liked the excitement of flying through the sky."

Maya wondered whether she was going to like flying too. Her insides felt wobbly as she kissed her parents and went to find Sophy and Clover.

They waited a long time by the bridge.

Then at last, just as the colour of dawn began creeping into the sky, the sound of wingbeats filled the air.

Sophy leapt up at once. "Windrunner, is that you?"

The noise grew louder and swirls of wind lifted the girls' hair. Windrunner landed in the river with an enormous splash. He paddled to the edge, climbed out and shook the water off his huge leathery wings. The girls stood back so that they didn't get soaked.

"Hello, Sophy! Hello, Maya!" Windrunner

looked at Clover with kind amber eyes. "Hello, little unicorn."

"Hello, Windrunner," said Maya. "It's great to see you."

Sophy ran up to give the dragon a hug. "Thank you for coming back."

Windrunner bowed his head. "Where to now, Sophy?"

"We're taking this foal back to the sky unicorn herd," Sophy told him.

Windrunner made Sophy stand back before giving out a long fiery breath to dry off his wet scales. "Climb on!"

Sophy and Maya scrambled on. Clover didn't
want to at first but Sophy explained that it
might be too far for him to fly. He found it hard
to balance on Windrunner's back, but the girls
helped him and soon they were all sitting down
safely. Maya's heart thumped as she held on
tight.

With a massive leap, Windrunner took off.
He soared high above the river before swooping
down till they almost touched the water. Rising
high again, he took them up and up until Maya
thought she could almost touch the clouds.

The Emerald Plain rolled past below them.
Maya gazed at the long, curving shape of the
river that she was so used to sailing on. It was
strange to see it from here – it looked so small!

The sky grew brighter as the sun rose.
Windrunner flew on steadily. Clover's eyelids
drooped and he slept for a while. Maya held
on to him, making sure he stayed safely on the
dragon's back.

"I can see the unicorn herd," Windrunner growled, plunging downwards.

The sky unicorns raised their heads as the storm dragon landed at the edge of their valley. One unicorn rushed forward, tossing her mane in delight.

Clover woke up and bounded down from the dragon's back to meet his mum again. They touched noses and then Clover's mum nibbled his ear.

Maya and Sophy climbed down more slowly
and the herd of sky unicorns gathered round
them.

"How strange that two girls and a storm
dragon have brought our little Clover back to
us," said one unicorn.

"Perhaps the stories from the songbirds are
true," said another. "Can you talk to us, girls?
Do you have a magical stone that makes this
possible?"

"Yes, we do!" said Maya.

Both girls took out their stones and showed the sky unicorns the beautiful crystals inside. The magical animals nodded their heads and murmured to each other.

"I thank you for bringing my baby back to me," said Clover's mum, and she bowed her head to each of the girls and then to Windrunner. "I think the human who took him must be a very bad man."

Windrunner shook his head, smoke billowing from his nostrils. "Sir Fitzroy is dangerous! What wicked ideas will he have next?"

"Then you haven't heard?" said Clover's mum. "The songbirds tell us he has sent letters to his friends all over the kingdom, urging them to capture magical animals. Every enchanted creature is now in danger."

Maya and Sophy exchanged looks.

"I won't let him hurt them," cried Sophy. "I'm going to find more people who will help – people who can use the Speaking Stones like Maya and me."

"I'll come with you!" said Maya. "We can't let Sir Fitzroy win. There are lots of different creatures to protect – star wolves, firebirds and

many more. We'll have to fly right across the kingdom!"

A unicorn with a pale-green tail stepped in front of Maya. "My name is Marella," she said. "I would like to repay the great help you have given young Clover by offering to carry you anywhere you wish to go."

"Thank you," said Maya. "I'd like that very much!" She climbed on to Marella's back.

Clover bounced up to them. "Don't forget to come back and visit me, Maya!"

"I won't!" Maya beamed down at him. "I could never forget you, Clover!"

Sophy climbed on to Windrunner's back. The storm dragon and the sky unicorn soared side by side into the light-blue sky.

Maya smiled across at Sophy. She couldn't wait for their next secret rescue!